This is an Em Querido book
Published by Levine Querido

LEVINE QUERIDO

www.levinequerido.com · info@levinequerido.com

Levine Querido is distributed by Chronicle Books LLC

Library of Congress Control Number: 2019953555
ISBN 978-1-64614-007-7

Printed and bound in Italy

Published in September 2020
First Printing

Book design by Christine Kettner
The text type was set in Truesdell

To create this book, the illustrator received a grant from the Creative Industries Fund NL.

LITTLE FOX

EDWARD VAN DE VENDEL & MARIJE TOLMAN

TRANSLATED BY DAVID COLMER

LEVINE QUERIDO

MONTCLAIR · AMSTERDAM · NEW YORK

Little Fox races along behind two butterflies.
Because they're purple.

Suddenly there's no ground under Little Fox's paws, only air!

Little Fox falls

and falls.

The ground rushes up
and hits him:
THUMP!

And then...

then his dream starts.

Little Fox has never had a dream like this before.

He is a baby again, as small as an apple.

It's dark.

He says, "Ee, ee."

And all he can think is mommy and milk, and milk and mommy, and mm mm mmm mm mm mm mmm.

The dream goes on.

Little Fox is a few weeks older.

He smells daddy fox.

He smells him coming into the den with a mouse in his jaws.

The mouse smells of –

it doesn't matter what the mouse smells of,
because fox brother has already grabbed it.
Little Fox climbs over fox brother,
and fox sister and another fox sister are climbing too.
They're all climbing over each other.
It's warm and funny,
and all the time fox brother's paw is poking into
Little Fox's ear.

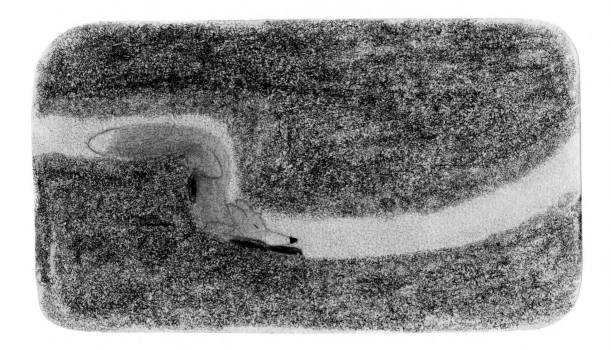

It's a beautiful dream.

Little Fox is a bit older again.

He goes outside for the first time, out of the den.

It's nighttime. There's a moon.

Little Fox doesn't know the moon yet.

He doesn't know that it looks like the sun, but silver.

He squeezes his eyes shut

until the moonlight stops stinging.

Then Little Fox jumps on his brother
and sisters and they jump on him, because
outside smells of everything all at once.

Of woods. Of moss.

 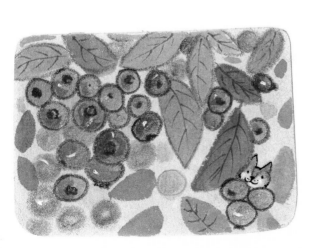

Of little animals (food)!

Of big animals (not food)!

Of grass and flowery flowers!

And when you stand in the wind your hair stands on end!

And when you turn around it blows the other way!

The dream keeps going.

It is still very early.

The sun has just risen. It's yawning in the sky.

Little Fox is thirsty.

The smell of fresh water always gives him a happy giddy feeling, so he runs towards it!

But there's a...
very big animal.
She's standing with her white bottom to Little Fox.
On legs like thin branches.
Little Fox hesitates for a moment, then creeps closer.
The animal has spots.
She also has very, very, very big ears.
She looks up.
She's not scared of Little Fox.
Why not?

Fox cubs can bite too, you know!
But Little Fox doesn't want to bite this animal.
He wants to drink some water.
And a little later that's what he does.
They drink water next to each other.
Birds are singing and the sun is now wide awake.

When the animal happens to turn her head towards him,
Little Fox sees a few drops of delicious water on her snout.
Is Little Fox brave enough? Yes, he is:

slurp –

he licks off the drops.

.

In the dream, daddy fox tells Little Fox
not to be so curious.
Daddy says, "Too nosy is dead nosy."
Little Fox doesn't understand.
But mommy and daddy know everything.
They show him how to be in the world.

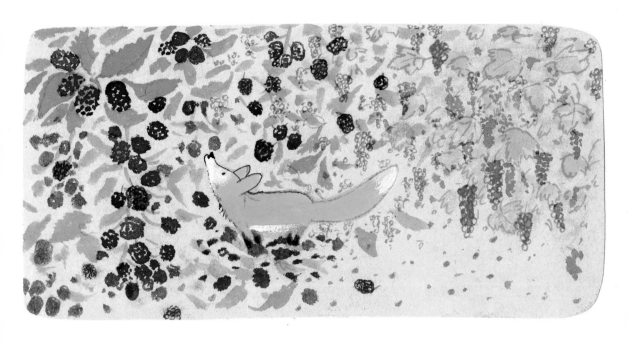

Blackberries and redcurrants – pick them with your lips.

A worm – jump on it.

Scuffle-mice – they're tricky.
First you have to hear them (stay nice and quiet),
then you have to grab them with your paws (they wriggle),
but then they make the yummiest noise of all.
They crunch between your jaws.
Oh, now Little Fox remembers what
his clever sister said once.
If you catch a mouse, it's because the mouse was
way too nosy.

The day with the ball!
That's in his dream too!
Little Fox runs off with his brother, because now
they're allowed to go further and further and
mommy doesn't get angry.

Suddenly a happy smell fills their noses.
The smell comes from a bag you can tear open
and if you root through it, you find lots of delicious
things, some sweet, some salty.
Their tongues get greedier and greedier.

The bag is next to the house
where the dangerous humans live.
And just when Little Fox and his brother
have finished eating,
they discover the ball.
Little Fox lies on his stomach.
That way he can get a good look at the ball-globe.

Then he jumps on it.

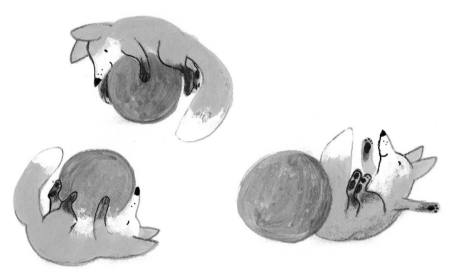

A ball is a sun on the ground.

The ball makes Little Fox forget everything.
His brother has already gone but that doesn't matter.
Little Fox keeps playing by himself.
He doesn't look up until he hears *click*.

It comes from one of the dangerous humans,
but it's a little one.
The little ones don't look dangerous.
And the little human has one big eye.
Click.
Just to be on the safe side, Little Fox runs off,
but first he does a quick pee on the ball.
That way his brother will know who was here last
if he comes back tomorrow.
Click.

The dream isn't all nice.

Oh-oh – now Little Fox sees that slippery nasty jar!

The slippery nasty jar was near the dangerous humans' house too.

Not far from the bag.

Not far from the ball.

The top of the jar looked like a hole,

so Little Fox stuck his head in it.

You often find food in holes – mice, rats, worms or moles – but there wasn't anything in the slippery nasty jar.

Just Little Fox's head.
And he couldn't get it out again.

He shook it.

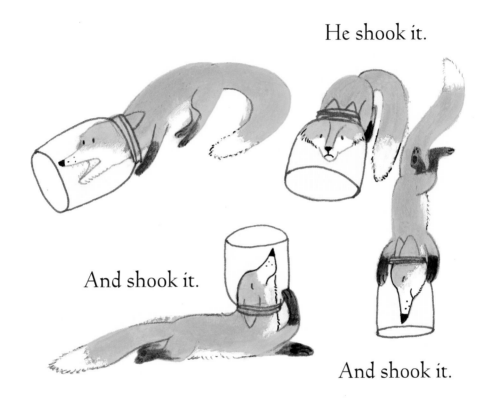

And shook it.

And shook it.

It didn't help.

He walked and ran and wriggled on the ground.

That didn't help either.

The jar got heavier. Little Fox thought,
why am I always so curious?

He hears daddy fox saying, "Too nosy is..."

But then he thinks, the human.

The little human with the big eye and the clicking sound.

And *phew...*

The little human helps.

What kind of dream is this?
First it seemed like it was only about nice things.
All the nice days he'd had.
But that day with that slippery jar – that wasn't nice.
And now Little Fox suddenly remembers what
mommy fox taught him:
that you have to curl up inside your tail
when it's cold,
or when the days are bad
and the world turns into an angry place.

Yes, what kind of dream is this?
Suddenly it's got two purple butterflies in it.
They are fluttering so happily that Little Fox runs along
behind them.

But then Little Fox is running in midair.
He falls
and the ground rushes up
and hits him with a
THUMP!

Little Fox sees himself lying there.

That's funny. It's not even possible.

You can only do things like that in dreams.

Little Fox sees Little Fox lying somewhere.

On the ground, in the sand.

He's not moving. His eyes are shut.

Little Fox thinks, how did things turn
out for that Little Fox?

He thinks, is that Little Fox going to wake up again?

And he thinks, hey, that Little Fox is me!

But then he smells something...
His fox brother and his fox sisters.
Mommy! Daddy!

Little Fox says to himself,
"I think I know how things turn out for that Little Fox.
I think that Little Fox opens his eyes
and everything's good."

And so Little Fox opens his eyes

because everything is good.

Isn't it? Oh no, wait,
Little Fox sees more butterflies.
But he is certainly not going to
chase them.

Because none of them are purple.

SOME NOTES ON THIS BOOK'S PRODUCTION

To make the art for the interiors and cover,
Marije Tolman took photos of the Dutch dunes and woods
and made risograph prints of them. Then, she used various techniques
to draw on the prints (gouache, watercolor, acrylic,
colored pencil, pen, ink and chalk).

The text was set in Truesdell, originally designed by Frederic Goudy
in 1930, revived by Steve Matteson for Monotype in 1994.
The display text was set in Montecatini Pro Stretto,
first released by Louise Fili Ltd in 2017.

This full-color book features a dazzling fifth color,
PMS 804 C orange. The case for the book is three pieces:
the front and the back are printed on 135 gsm wood free paper with
a matt laminate, and the spine is real cloth, colored Brilianta 4032.
The book was printed on 150 gsm GardaMatt art coated
FSC-certified paper and bound in Italy.

Production was supervised by Leslie Cohen and Freesia Blizard
Book jacket and interiors designed by Christine Kettner
Edited by Arthur A. Levine

Thanks to Ramon, Mees, Liv and Wolf for the walks through the dunes of The Hague,
Wassenaar, Katwijk, Langevelderslag, Texel, Vlieland and Terschelling. Marije